米亞與艾瑪
MIA AND EMMA

陳聖蕾 Mia Chen／著

米亞和艾瑪是一對相差兩歲的姐妹，
姐姐米亞害羞內斂，
妹妹艾瑪活潑調皮。
她們吵架，鬧彆扭，
但這並不妨礙她們始終是最好的朋友。
她們與爸爸媽媽的日常平凡有趣，
吵吵鬧鬧的一起長大。

目 錄

1 艾瑪的新水壺

　　晚飯後，爸爸媽媽領著米亞和艾瑪去家附近的百貨超市轉轉。晚上的百貨超市沒什麼人，於是媽媽便允許米亞和艾瑪可以自己在超市裡逛。

　　「我想去看看這裡有沒有好看的手帕，老師說幼兒園的每個小朋友都得帶自己的手帕。」米亞對艾瑪說。

　　「我也要去！」艾瑪蹦蹦跳跳的跟在姐姐身後，姊妹倆　前　後穿過裝拖鞋的人籃筐，展示沙發椅子的區域，最後終於到了擺放家居用品的地方。

　　「我喜歡這個粉色帶有人蝴蝶結，但是這個紫色貓咪的也很好看，我都不知道該選哪個了。」米亞手裡拿著兩條手帕，糾結著不知道該選哪一條。

　　就在這時米亞發現本來跟在自己身後的妹妹不見了，於是放下印有小貓咪圖案的手帕開始找起了艾瑪。

　　噠噠噠，噠噠噠……腳步聲從米亞後面傳來，艾瑪出現在身後，手裡抱著一個比她的頭還要大上不少的水壺。

米亞與艾瑪

「我要這個水壺！」艾瑪大聲宣布。

「妳需要先問問媽媽同不同意才行。」米亞向妹妹潑了一桶冷水。艾瑪的大眼睛往左轉了兩圈，又往右轉了兩圈，便扭頭走了。

「喂！等等我！」米亞緊跟在艾瑪身後。米亞跟著妹妹在賣場裡繞啊繞，直到艾瑪突然向前跑去⋯⋯原來她一直在找媽媽。

「我要這個水壺，非常需要！」艾瑪將水壺抱得更緊。

艾瑪的新水壺

「家裡已經有很多水壺了，而且這個水壺對妳來說太大太重了，快把水壺放回去，我們準備要回家了。」

「我就要這個水壺！」

眼淚啪嗒啪嗒從艾瑪眼裡流出來。

「就要！」

每當艾瑪想要什麼東西的時候，她總是態度堅定，不容置疑，不達目的絕不罷休的。

艾瑪的哭鬧聲很快引來了爸爸，爸爸的出現讓艾瑪更激動了。她邊哭邊踩腳，不管爸爸媽媽怎麼說都沒有用，艾瑪的眼淚像瀑布一樣不停的從眼睛裡往外流，後來鼻涕口水也止不住的流出來。。

無奈之下最終爸爸媽媽還是給艾瑪買了那個大水壺，當然還有米亞的蝴蝶結手帕。回家的路上艾瑪心滿意足的抱著她的新水壺走了一路。

第二天從幼兒園放學回家後，只看見艾瑪怒氣沖沖的把外套書包掛好後，自己搬了一把椅子，踩著它夠到了廚房裡的櫥櫃，把新水壺擺到了櫃子的最深處，砰的一聲又把櫃門關上了。

「妳怎麼把水壺收起來了呀？」米亞好奇的問道。

艾瑪噘起嘴來，一聲不吭進了自己的房間後，向門外吼了一聲：「我再也不要那個水壺了！不要了！」

米亞帶著疑惑去找媽媽，只看見媽媽又把新水壺從櫃子裡拿了出來。

「艾瑪說她再也不要帶這個水壺去上學了，爲什麼呀？」米亞問媽媽。

「老師說今天在班上大家喝水的時候，艾瑪的水壺實在太大太重了，在她舉起水壺喝水時，水壺砸在了她的臉上，水灑出來把她最喜歡的小狗上衣弄濕了。」

說到這裡，媽媽忍不住笑了出來，「看來這個水壺只能等艾瑪再大一點才能用了。」

　　原來是這樣！米亞終於明白了。想著去艾瑪房間找
她玩過家家，米亞推開了艾瑪房間的門，只看見艾瑪嘴
裡叼著奶瓶，縮成一團躺在床上睡著了。

　　看來這一天這支水壺給艾瑪添了不少麻煩。

米亞與艾瑪

2 老師遊戲

　　一天放學後，米亞和艾瑪決定要一起玩她們最喜歡的遊戲。這個遊戲首先要有一個老師，再來要有教室，教室裡要有書桌，椅子，書本以及文具，最重要的是要有上課的學生。

　　「今天我來當老師！我今天剛在幼兒園學了一個新的舞蹈，所以我來當老師。」米亞對艾瑪說。

　　「那我也要當老師！老師今天在幼兒園教我們扭屁股。」艾瑪說著便扭起屁股來。

「不行，一個班上只能有一個老師。而且如果我們都是老師的話，誰來當聽課的學生呢？」米亞挺直腰桿嚴肅的對艾瑪說。「我比妳大，我是幼稚園大班的學生，是幼稚園裡最大的，所以我最適合當老師。」米亞接著補充。

　　「不公平！」艾瑪跺腳吼道。眼看著妹妹就要爆發了，米亞決定還是和平玩遊戲最重要，於是她提出輪流當老師，最後再決定誰才是最合格的老師。艾瑪這才冷靜下來，也同意姐姐的提議。

　　「那就讓我來當老師教跳舞和數數，艾瑪妳先當班上的學生。」

　　艾瑪似懂非懂地點點頭。

　　接著米亞和艾瑪開始搭起她們的教室。首先要從餐桌那邊扚椅子搬進房間裡來，接著要從儲藏間拿些紙箱做桌子，然後要從爸爸的書房借塊小白板和幾支筆和紙。最後還得換上適合上學還有唱歌跳舞的服裝，公主裙再適合不過啦。

　　「好極了，現在我們是公主學院的老師和學生了！」米亞忍不住在原地轉起圈，低頭看著裙子，一下一下的鼓起來。

「好的，現在我們開始上課了。今天我要來教同學們怎麼像公主一樣跳舞，首先妳要像我一樣可以不停的在原地轉圈圈，至少要轉十圈。」說道米亞便又轉起圈來。

艾瑪看著姐姐不停的轉圈也跟著一塊轉了起來，直到頭暈後兩姐妹躺在地上，抬頭看著屋頂的天花板還在不停的轉。

「現在該學數數了，我們來從一數到一百，我先數二十個數字然後妳再重複我數的。」說罷米亞便從一數到了二十。

「好了，現在該換妳數了。」

「一，二，三……」艾瑪扳著手指頭數數，但數到十以後艾瑪發現手指頭不夠用了。「我不想數數了，數數不好玩！」艾瑪鼓著小臉對姐姐說。「現在換我當老師了！」

2 老師遊戲

「但是我們還沒有數完呢，現在才剛數到二十。」

「我現在就妛當老師！」艾瑪看起來非常生氣，眉毛都皺到了一塊去。米亞看著艾瑪一臉殺氣的瞪著自己，不自覺地往後倒退了兩步……「妳幹嘛往後退？我又不是鬼！」於是米亞又小心翼翼地回到了原來的位置。接著艾瑪走到了白板前，開始一步一步把今天老師

米亞與艾瑪

教的扭屁股向米亞示範。米亞跟著扭了兩下後便雙手叉腰站在原地。

「好了我學會了，現在我們應該繼續學數數了。」米亞對艾瑪說。

「不公平！妳當了那麼久老師我才只當了一下下，而且我的扭屁股妳還沒有學完！」

「我不想學了，扭屁股好幼稚！而且我才是真正的老師！」米亞吼著。

「我才是！」艾瑪嗓門更大。

「不許吵架！再吵架今天誰也不許再玩遊戲了！」媽媽進了房間對米亞和艾瑪說。「妳們兩個都是很棒的老師，妳們兩個為什麼不能一起當老師呢？」

「我們兩個都當老師的話，那誰來當我們的學生呢？」米亞問媽媽。媽媽笑了笑走出房間，一會又回來了，只不過這次她的手裡多了幾個毛絨娃娃。「就讓小狗，小熊，小豬和洋娃娃當妳們的學生怎麼樣？妳們兩個可以一塊教他們。」說完，媽媽把娃娃們擺好一排坐在椅子上。「我敢保證他們一定是最聽話的學生。」

2 老師遊戲

「那我們先一起教他們扭屁股，然後再教數學，妳覺得怎麼樣？」米亞問妹妹。

「我覺得這樣很好。」艾瑪回答道。

米亞與艾瑪

3 動物園的表演

今天幼兒園小班的小朋友們要在動物園裡演出，當然這其中就包括了艾瑪。今天是個重要的日子，於是全家一大早吃完早餐後就向幼兒園出發。

「爲什麼艾瑪不跟我們一起走？她去哪了？」米亞問道。

「艾瑪和班上老師和其他小朋友一起搭學校的巴士先去動物園了，他們要先去換服裝還要彩排，所以一大早就出發了。」媽媽回答。

米亞坐在車裡看著窗外的雲朵想像著動物園裡的各種動物，有大象，長頸鹿，還有河馬。想到這裡米亞更迫不及待了。

「我們到得很早，所以可以先在動物園裡轉轉，艾瑪的演出中午才開始，我們還有很多時間。」爸爸對米亞說道。

「太好了！我們可以先去看看無尾熊嗎？」

「當然可以。」

　　到了動物園後，爸爸媽媽領著米亞去看了好多動物，有袋鼠、無尾熊、長頸鹿、大象，還有可愛的熊貓。到中午的時候爸爸還給米亞買了雞蛋布丁，每次來動物園都要吃。米亞特別留了一個布丁打算等艾瑪表演完後給她。接著爸爸媽媽帶著米亞去位於動物園中心的演播廳，艾瑪的表演就要開始了。

很快，舞臺的簾幕拉開了，十幾個小企鵝排排站成一列，其中就有艾瑪。

　　「艾瑪是小企鵝呀！」米亞驚嘆的對媽媽說。

　　「很可愛對吧？」媽媽說完，便舉起相機對著舞臺上的小企鵝們喀嚓喀嚓的拍起照片。

　　隨著音樂響起，小企鵝們搖搖晃晃的在舞臺上轉圈，揮手，扭屁股。只不過艾瑪這隻小企鵝永遠比別的小企鵝慢半拍，眼睛還不停的在觀眾席飄忽。

　　「媽媽，艾瑪好像在找我們，她看不見我們嗎？」米亞擔心的問媽媽。

　　「舞臺上的燈太亮了，所以看不見觀眾，妳可以試著跟艾瑪揮揮手讓她知道我們在觀眾席看她。」媽媽悄悄在米亞耳邊說道。聽完媽媽的話，米亞立馬興奮的向舞臺不停招手，直到艾瑪看見臺下的姐姐，她才終於露出笑容。但麻煩的是艾瑪不跳舞了，站在原地不停的向觀眾席的姐姐招手，蹦蹦跳跳的鼓掌。

　　「媽媽妳看，艾瑪看見我了，她在和我招手呢！」米亞興奮的跟媽媽說。

3 動物園的表演

「哦～我的天！」

　　艾瑪這隻小企鵝完全忘記了表演，她身邊的小企
鵝做動作換位置的時候都要拉她一把、推她一下、帶著
她轉個圈圈……艾瑪就像個小木偶一樣被別的小朋友牽
一下動一下，目光始終望著台下的姐姐，小手不停地揮
著。台下的觀眾被逗得笑成一片。

　　就這樣，演出在米亞和艾瑪的互相招手中結束了。

3 動物園的表演

4 最糟糕的一天

　　媽媽出差了，這次米亞和艾瑪要單獨和爸爸度過一個禮拜的時間。米亞並不喜歡這樣，她喜歡有媽媽在家裡。媽媽知道米亞上學喜歡帶有蝴蝶結的手帕，媽媽知道米亞上學喜歡紮兩個麻花辮，媽媽知道每個禮拜五米亞都可以穿漂亮的小花裙子去上學，最重要的是，每天早上一睜眼米亞和艾瑪就能喝到媽媽剛泡好的熱牛奶。這些都是爸爸不知道的。

　　星期五早晨，米亞和艾瑪起床後發現床邊的牛奶居然是涼的，而且爸爸還用米亞的奶瓶泡艾瑪的牛奶，用艾瑪的奶瓶泡米亞的牛奶。「哦！還能比這更糟嗎？」喝完不太好喝的牛奶，米亞下床去找爸爸幫忙自己換衣服。米亞特別跟爸爸強調今天是星期五，是穿小花裙子的日子。不過爸爸卻向米亞道歉說小花裙子還在洗衣機裡，今天不能穿。最後爸爸給米亞穿上了最不喜歡的灰色運動褲和一件沒有小花或亮片的上衣。「哦！我的天，還能比這更糟嗎？」此時的米亞無比想念出差中的媽媽。

換完衣服以後，米亞跟爸爸說要紮兩個麻花辮。爸爸卻說他並不會紮米亞喜歡的麻花辮，只是簡單的幫米亞紮了一個馬尾。「我相信今天不會更糟了！」米亞有些生氣的說道。

　　到了學校後，老師要求同學們洗完手後要拿出手帕把手擦乾。就在這時米亞發現，爸爸裝錯手帕了。口袋裡拿出的並不是帶有蝴蝶結的手帕，而是一條米亞最討厭的紅色手帕。「今天真的是最糟糕的一天！」

下午爸爸來接米亞和艾瑪放學，只看見米亞從學校出來後就一直皺眉頭還嘟著嘴，一句話也不說。爸爸有些困惑地問：「妳看上去好像有點不開心？能告訴爸爸是為什麼嗎？」說完，米亞的眼淚突然不爭氣的從眼眶裡啪嗒啪嗒止不住地往外流。「我想媽媽了。」米亞再也忍不住了，她多麼希望明天一早起來就能喝到媽媽泡的熱牛奶，能梳媽媽紮的麻花辮，能從口袋裡拿出蝴蝶結圖案的手帕。

　　爸爸蹲下來面對米亞說：「我們去買冰淇淋吃吧？」爸爸牽著一路不停抹鼻涕和眼淚的米亞，和只要聽見冰淇淋就無比興奮一路上蹦蹦跳跳的艾瑪去了學校附近的便利商店，爸爸給我們三個人每人買了一枝香草冰淇淋。回家的路上，米亞和艾瑪一邊舔著冰淇淋，一邊跟爸爸分享今天在學校發生的趣事。這時，米亞注意到爸爸腳上穿著兩隻不是一對的襪子，連顏色都不一樣。看來媽媽不在家裡，爸爸連自己都照顧不好。

　　「今天不糟糕了，因為有好吃的冰淇淋，還有穿錯襪子的爸爸。」米亞心裡這麼決定。

4 最糟糕的一天

5 萬聖節

今天是一年一度的萬聖節，米亞和艾瑪很興奮。在這天學校裡的老師和同學都會裝扮起來，這也包括米亞和艾瑪。

「我今年的服裝是仙女，媽媽給我新買了一條漂亮的仙女裙，還有翅膀呢！」米亞對艾瑪說。艾瑪也期待換上了自己的小狗服裝，是她自己選的，她等不及能變成一隻真正的小狗了！

「妳的小狗會飛嗎？」米亞問艾瑪。艾瑪想了想回答：「會！」

「不，妳不會，因為妳沒有翅膀，也沒有仙女棒來施展魔法。」米亞得意的對艾瑪說。艾瑪不太開心了。

「我會飛，我就會飛！」艾瑪生氣的對姐姐說。

「妳當然不會，因為妳沒有被撒上精靈粉。」米亞揮舞著手裡的仙女棒，在艾瑪的頭上繞了好幾個圈。

「現在妳會飛了，因為我給妳撒了一些精靈粉。」說著米亞用魔法棒輕輕的點了一下艾瑪的頭頂。

艾瑪閉上眼睛，仰起小臉笑着，好像真的感受到了精靈粉的魔力。

「現在我們可以一起飛了，我們要飛著去要糖。」米亞跟艾瑪說，「準備好了嗎？」艾瑪像搗蒜一樣地點頭。

「我準備好吃很多的糖果了。」艾瑪開心地回答道。

「真希望能有大塊的巧克力，那樣的話這個萬聖節就會是最完美的萬聖節。」米亞在心裡默默祈禱著。

接著爸爸就送米亞和艾瑪去上學。她們已經等不及晚上的時候去要糖了！

5 萬聖節

6 艾瑪的時髦瀏海

　　米亞從幼稚園帶了手工作業回家。一回到家她就向艾瑪宣布，她今天要完成手工作業，不能跟艾瑪一起玩了！說完她就回到房間，為防止艾瑪進去搗亂，她還關上了房門，把艾瑪關在了門外邊。

　　現在，沒有了姐姐一起玩，艾瑪一個人無聊地在沙發上滾來滾去、滾上滾下。

　　我們都知道，艾瑪的小腦袋裡永遠有層出不窮的點子，這會兒不知道她又想到了什麼，只見她在沙發上滾了一半忽然停住了，發了一陣子呆，然後起身去她的玩具廚房裡拿了一個塑料小碗，去爸爸的書房拿了剪刀，最後去自己的房間找到了一面小鏡子。接著艾瑪便回到了沙發前的茶几那裡，把鏡子擺好後，一手拿起剪刀，另一手端起塑料小碗開始給自己變身。

　　她認真地剪起自己的瀏海，手上端著的小碗正好接住自己剪下的碎頭髮。

「哦我的天吶！艾瑪妳的瀏海！」媽媽驚呼。

「怎麼了，發生什麼事了？」聽見屋外的聲響，米亞好奇的跑到客廳想一探究竟。

　　原來艾瑪給自己的瀏海剪了一個正方形的洞。被媽媽發現時，艾瑪還在認真的給自己修剪剩下的瀏海。

　　媽媽忍不住笑了起來「這簡直太好玩了，艾瑪真的給自己剪了一個非常時髦的頭髮。」米亞也忍不住笑了起來。看見媽媽和姐姐笑的眼淚都快流出來了，艾瑪的臉頰頓時變得像蘋果一樣紅通通的，自己也忍不住咯咯的笑起來。

　　也許我真的非常適合當一個理髮師，艾瑪在心裡想著。

7 吃雞蛋

　　米亞和艾瑪很煩惱。每天早上，媽媽都會給姐妹倆每人煮兩顆雞蛋當做早餐，並且告訴她們，雞蛋最有營養，如果要想長高，就一定要把自己的兩顆雞蛋吃完，否則就沒有甜點可以吃。

　　「我討厭吃蛋黃，蛋黃讓我覺得我在吃小雞寶寶。」米亞懊惱的說。

　　「我討厭吃蛋白。」艾瑪也皺著眉頭嘟囔道「蛋白什麼味道都沒有，一點也不好吃。」

　　「這下該怎麼辦？」米亞擔憂的看著妹妹「媽媽說了，不把雞蛋吃完的話就不能吃小蛋糕了。」

　　艾瑪的喉嚨發出咕嚕咕嚕的聲音，小腦袋卻不停的轉呀轉，努力的想出一個能不吃討厭的蛋白，但又能吃到小蛋糕的辦法。

　　雖然萬般不喜歡，但米亞總是一邊抱怨著，一邊還是乖乖把雞蛋都吃掉。每每這時，艾瑪總是安靜的一聲不響。

7吃雞蛋

日子就這樣一天天過去了，忽然有一天，媽媽在整理房間的時候，在艾瑪的廚房玩具櫃裡發現了滿滿一鍋發霉的蛋白。

　　原來，每天米亞艱難地吃掉全部雞蛋的時候，艾瑪都是悄悄地把自己討厭吃的蛋白藏起來了，她以為只要藏起來了，蛋白就不存在了，沒想到那些蛋白不會自己消失，而是發霉了，最終還是被媽媽發現了。

媽媽很生氣，每天檢查艾瑪的雞蛋全部吃掉了才能離開餐桌。艾瑪發脾氣也沒用，媽媽絕不妥協。艾瑪也不妥協，她的小腦袋一刻不停地想著對付媽媽的辦法。她看著姐姐飛快地吃掉了蛋白，趕緊悄悄地把自己蛋白放到了姐姐的盤子裡。

米亞生氣地叫了一聲「艾瑪！」正要向媽媽告狀，卻忽然想到了什麼，「我知道了！」米亞突然興奮的拍了拍艾瑪。「我幫妳把妳討厭的蛋白吃掉，妳幫我把我討厭的蛋黃吃掉，這樣不就好了嗎！」。

艾瑪不得不承認，這是一個非常完美的主意。 這樣一來，她可以不用吃討厭的蛋白，卻又可以吃到小蛋糕。

「就這麼辦！」艾瑪悄悄的在姐姐耳邊說。

7吃雞蛋

就這樣，米亞吃了四顆雞蛋的蛋白，艾瑪吃了四顆蛋黃。艾瑪嘴裡還塞滿了蛋黃就已經迫不及待的叫「媽媽，媽媽！我們吃完雞蛋了！現在可以給我們吃小蛋糕了嗎？」

　　「真的都吃完了！妳們真棒。」媽媽誇獎米亞艾瑪。「現在妳們可以一人吃一塊小蛋糕了。」

　　最終，艾瑪和米亞成功完成了媽媽設下的不可能任務，姐妹倆無比享受地吃起了美味的小蛋糕。

8 米亞的生日禮物

　　今天是個特別的日子，因爲今天是米亞的生日。米亞最喜歡過生日了，在這天不光有好吃的生日蛋糕，姥姥、姥爺、舅舅、舅媽、小姨、小姨夫都會來給米亞慶祝生日！最重要的是，媽媽還會給米亞買一個特別的生日禮物。

　　爲了這特別的一天，米亞早早的就換上了心愛的小花裙子，還搭配好了要穿的鞋子。現在就等媽媽說可以出門了！媽媽要先帶米亞去商場買生日禮物，晚上再和大家一起吹生日蠟燭，吃生日蛋糕。米亞等不及了！

　　出門時，艾瑪那個小跟屁蟲一定要跟著，不管米亞怎麼反對，讓她留在家裏，她都固執地跟出了門。到了商場，米亞領著媽媽直奔頂樓的玩具區。剛走沒兩步，米亞就拉著媽媽進了賣芭比娃娃的商店。

　　「這裡到處都是芭比娃娃，是芭比娃娃天堂！」說完米亞就鬆開媽媽的手，自己在店裡逛了起來。

過了一會兒媽媽找到蹲在店最裡面的米亞，問她「怎麼樣呀？這裡有妳喜歡的生日禮物嗎？」

米亞舉起剛才一直在看的芭比娃娃禮盒，裡面不光有一只芭比娃娃，還有好幾套漂亮的衣服和裙子，還有灑滿亮粉的包包和小貓。

「我想要這個當我的生日禮物！」米亞對媽媽說。

米亞與艾瑪

「沒問題。」說完，媽媽就帶著米亞去結賬了。店員把芭比娃娃放進一個漂亮的粉色袋子，還繫上了一個大大的粉色蝴蝶結，米亞婉拒了媽媽提出的要幫她拎袋子的好意。米亞要自己拎著漂亮袋子。

艾瑪羨慕地看著，眼睛都亮了，她問姐姐；她可以和姐姐一起玩嗎？她只要玩芭比的那隻小貓就好。米亞想了想，大方地說當然可以。

下樓時，經過賣服裝的樓層，米亞一眼就看見了她夢寐以求的公主裙，她走過去，站在那件裙子前面走不動了。

「哦不，我該怎麼辦！」米亞忽然覺得公主裙比芭比娃娃更適合當生日禮物。米亞跟媽媽說：「我覺得公主裙比芭比娃娃更適合當生日禮物」媽媽說沒問題，可以把芭比娃娃換成公主裙。

米亞猶豫了，「但是我還是非常喜歡芭比娃娃的。」

8 米亞的生日禮物

媽媽讓米亞自己好好想一想到底想要哪一個，米亞好爲難呀！

艾瑪看著米亞問，「姐姐妳很喜歡那個裙子哦？」

米亞根本沒有心思理會艾瑪的問話，她的心思在芭比娃娃和公主裙之間糾結著。

不知過了多久，米亞終於做了決定，她牽起媽媽的手，「我希望明年的生日我能買這條公主裙當生日禮物。」

米亞與艾瑪

「當然可以，明年生日媽媽送妳這條公主裙。」

說完，媽媽領著失落的米亞前往餐廳。

到了餐廳後，米亞驚喜的發現椅子上居然放了一個漂亮的紙袋子，上面還畫了蝴蝶結。「快拆開，快拆開！」艾瑪拉著姐姐到袋子面前。米亞驚訝地發現袋子裡居然是那條公主裙！

「這是艾瑪送給妳的。」媽媽開心的跟米亞說。

原來，當米亞站在商場裡，在芭比娃娃與公主裙之間猶豫不定的時候，艾瑪走到店員面前，吃力地從自己的口袋裏掏出一枚硬幣，高高地舉起並遞給店員，說她要買那條裙子送給姐姐。

店員被艾瑪的小樣子給逗笑了，媽媽也看見了艾瑪的舉動，她衝著店員使了眼色，店員會意，她高興地接過艾瑪的硬幣，拿了一條新裙子出來，替艾瑪包好，放進了媽媽的購物袋裡。當然最後是媽媽悄悄地把錢付給了店員。

8 米亞的生日禮物

　　「這簡直是最完美的生日了！」米亞抱起艾瑪不停
的轉圈圈，艾瑪笑得更開心了。

　　後來，姥姥、姥爺、舅舅、舅媽、小姨、小姨丈都
來陪米亞一起吃蛋糕，吹蠟燭，過了一個完美的生日。

9 小雞寶寶

　　媽媽在跟姥姥打電話，因為今天家裡收到了姥姥送來的一箱小雞寶寶。大大的紙箱裡一共有四隻小雞。米亞和艾瑪興奮極了，她們從來沒有養過寵物，當然也從來沒有養過小雞當寵物。

　　從小雞進家門開始，米亞和艾瑪的眼睛就沒有離開過牠們，四隻手也從來沒從裝小雞的箱子放下過。「我想摸摸牠們。」艾瑪說。

「可以，但是妳得輕輕的。」米亞對妹妹說，「不然妳會嚇到牠們的。」

艾瑪小心的用手輕輕摸著小雞的後背。突然，艾瑪抓起其中一只小雞的翅膀。

「不，妳不能這樣做！」米亞驚呼「妳會弄疼牠的！」

艾瑪手裡的小雞揮了揮翅膀從艾瑪手裡掙脫出來。晚上爸爸回家時發現米亞和艾瑪還圍在裝小雞的箱子旁專心的觀察裡頭的小雞。「看來妳們很喜歡小雞們呢。」爸爸對米亞艾瑪說。

米亞轉頭面對爸爸問：「我們能不能給牠們換一個家？紙箱裡都是小雞的便便，牠們非常需要一個乾淨的新家。」

「的確是這樣。」爸爸看了看箱子裡的小雞。「妳們等我一下。」過了一會爸爸抱著一個比紙箱大上不少的塑料盆從房間裡走出來，他說：「就拿這個給小雞做新家吧！」

隔天早上，爸爸媽媽，米亞艾瑪都眼睛都變得跟熊貓一樣。原來，昨天晚上小雞不停的吱吱叫，還自己從盆子裡跳出來，在家裡到處趴趴走，還隨地拉便便。全家人都被吵得睡不著，半夜起來抓小雞，爸爸媽媽還要清理地上的便便。

「今天還得去幼兒園呢，快打起精神來。」媽媽對還睡眼惺忪的兩姐妹說。不過想到放學回來就能和小雞一起玩，米亞艾瑪還是乖乖的出發去了幼兒園。

放學回家後，米亞艾瑪迫不及待的脫鞋，洗手，想著快點能跟小雞玩。結果發現裝小雞的塑料盆卻是空的。

「小雞不見了！」她以為小雞又自己從盆裡逃走了，趴在地上到處張望，想找到小雞。

「不用找了，媽媽今天把小雞送去農場了，小雞不能再住在家裡了，牠們在那裏會更開心。」媽媽說。

「為什麼？為什麼要把小雞送走！」艾瑪不理解的大叫，眼裡堆滿了淚珠。

9 小雞寶寶

「我們家不適合養小雞」媽媽接著說：「小雞們每天都在長大，很快牠們會希望能在更廣闊的地方活動，所以呀，媽媽送牠們去農場，那裡牠們可以自由自在的活動。」

　　「真的嗎？」米亞問不確定的問媽媽：「牠們不會被吃掉嗎？」

　　媽媽笑著回答：「農場是媽媽朋友自己的農場，保證不會把小雞吃掉。而且過幾天放假我們還可以去農場看小雞們。」

　　說到這裡，米亞和艾瑪的臉上總算露出笑容。她們跟媽媽拉勾保證一定要去看小雞後，就開開心心的去給每隻小雞畫一幅畫，打算下次去看牠們的時候帶給牠們。

10 花市

　　每個週末的早上，米亞和艾瑪都要陪阿公去逛花市。米亞和艾瑪很喜歡逛花市，因為花市裡不僅有花，還有很多好玩的小東西，比如一些做工精美的小飾物、小擺設，還有各式各樣的玩具，有漂亮的瓷娃娃，有可愛的小動物，對了對了，還有艾瑪最喜歡的小金魚。當然最最重要的是，每次去花市，阿公都會讓米亞和艾瑪各選一件自己喜歡的東西，然後買給她們。

　　在去花市的路上，米亞和艾瑪就開始討論這一次要收穫什麼寶貝，米亞問艾瑪想好要買什麼了嗎？艾瑪想說什麼卻又憋了回去，嘟起小嘴搖了搖頭。米亞學著大人的樣子無奈地笑笑，說，「艾瑪妳總是這麼沒主意可不行。」

　　花市人山人海，米亞和艾瑪緊緊牽著爺爺的手。「想看什麼要跟爺爺說哦。」

　　「我想去看看金魚！」艾瑪拉著爺爺的衣角往金魚的攤位前去。

10 花市

　　金魚的攤位不光有金魚還有各式各樣用來裝飾魚缸的擺飾。有小房子，有不同形狀和顏色的珊瑚，還有用玻璃做的小鯨魚。最後，米亞看見掛在鐵架子上各種形狀圖案的水晶寶寶。

　　「阿公，我想要那只紅色的小金魚！」艾瑪一只手拽著阿公的衣角，一只手指著魚缸裡的金魚。還沒等阿公說話，米亞搶著說「艾瑪不行，妳不能買金魚！」

米亞與艾瑪

艾瑪呆呆地看著姐姐，有些委屈地小聲說：「可是我想要魚魚……」

米亞堅定地說不可以！

阿公不明白，問為什麼？

米亞說因為艾瑪會殺死牠的。

原來，因為艾瑪從小就喜歡魚，所以在艾瑪生日的時候，米亞讓媽媽替她買了一條藍色的小魚送給艾瑪做生日禮物。艾瑪很喜歡那條小魚，給牠起名叫小藍，無論到哪裡都要帶著小藍。就連去好朋友家過夜，艾瑪也堅持帶著小藍一起去。媽媽怕路上顛簸，水會灑出來，就給裝小藍的玻璃瓶罩了一層保鮮膜，囑咐艾瑪到了朋友家把保鮮膜拿掉就好了，結果艾瑪見到朋友們後便把媽媽的囑咐忘得一乾二淨了，把小藍放到一邊就去玩了，等晚上想起小藍的時候，小藍已經浮在水面一動不動了……

阿公聽完小藍的故事，看著艾瑪故意沉重地說：「原來是這樣啊……」

米亞對艾瑪說：「妳可以選一個玻璃做的小鯨魚，

10花市

也很漂亮啊。」

艾瑪小聲地嘟囔著：「可是我想要真的魚。」

阿公笑著對姐妹倆說：「阿公覺得艾瑪不會再犯同樣的錯誤了，現在艾瑪比那個時候又長大了一點，更懂事了，我們再給艾瑪一次機會，看看她會不會把小魚養好。」

艾瑪仰起小臉衝著阿公拼命點頭，阿公笑著對艾瑪說：「阿公知道了，那我們就選一條漂亮的金魚吧。」

接著他扭頭問米亞：「姐姐喜歡什麼呢？」還沒等米亞回答，阿公就被艾瑪拉著去看金魚從魚缸裡被撈出來。

最終米亞挑了一個精緻的小房子，放在魚缸裡的那種。「是個非常漂亮的小洋房。」阿公對米亞說。米亞也這麼覺得，她打算回家後把小房子擺在金魚的魚缸裡。這樣一來每天看魚的時候都可以看到。

最後在一個賣花的攤位前，米亞幫阿公選了一盆粉色的小花，艾瑪選了一盆黃色的。阿公說回家後要把這些花種在前院。

回家的路上，艾瑪捧起裝金魚的玻璃瓶說：「姐姐，我們給牠起名叫小橘好不好？」

二 吃餃子

姥姥家在北京，春節的習俗是除夕夜跨年時要吃餃子。

除夕這一天，吃過年夜飯之後，媽媽和姥姥就在廚房裡為夜裡的餃子做準備。姥姥負責擀麵團，媽媽負責做肉餡。米亞和艾瑪也想幫忙。

「我們可以做些什麼呢？」米亞和艾瑪問姥姥。姥姥放下擀麵杖看著姐妹倆臉上露出了微笑說：「讓我想想，有什麼能讓妳們幫忙的呢……」米亞和艾瑪期待地等在姥姥身旁。

突然，姥姥拍手說：「我知道了，妳們去幫我找些硬幣吧！」

「為什麼要找硬幣？」米亞好奇的問。

「晚點妳就知道了。」姥姥神祕兮兮的說。

於是艾瑪和米亞開始認真的在家裡搜羅硬幣。她們在沙發底下找到了一枚硬幣，又在鋼琴後面找到一枚，「我的綠色蠟筆原來在這！」沒錯，鋼琴後面還找到了艾瑪的綠色蠟筆。最後，她們又在爸爸的外套口袋裡找到了兩枚硬幣。

11 吃餃子

「妳們在找什麼？」爸爸突然出現在米亞艾瑪身後問道。「姥姥需要硬幣，我們全部都找過了，可是只找到了這幾個。」說完米亞和艾瑪伸出握著硬幣的手給爸爸看。

爸爸接著說：「我想我可以幫妳們，不過以後妳們可不能再隨便翻大人衣服的口袋。」

米亞艾瑪點頭答應。爸爸從書房裡拿出一隻陶瓷的小豬，小豬的肚子那裡有一個小洞。搖了兩下，就有好幾枚硬幣從小豬的肚子裡掉出來。

「哇！好多硬幣！」艾瑪米亞感到非常驚喜，姊妹倆手裡瞬間握滿了錢幣。

「這些應該夠了，再多妳們也拿不了，妳們說對吧？」爸爸說的對，哪怕是再多一枚硬幣，米亞和艾瑪的手也拿不下了。

把硬幣交給姥姥，姥姥卻讓米亞和艾瑪把硬幣好好洗一洗，要洗得特別乾淨才行。米亞和艾瑪從來沒有洗過硬幣，覺得好玩極了，把硬幣洗了一遍又一遍，直到姥姥說可以了，才把硬幣從水裡撈出來，放在紙巾上

晾乾。做完這些，爸爸就領著米亞與艾瑪出門去放鞭炮了。

　　終於到了吃餃子的時候，一盤盤熱騰騰的餃子擺在餐桌上。米亞和艾瑪等不及了！等大家碰杯後，年夜飯就正式開始了。米亞剛吃完第一顆餃子，就聽見小姨驚喜的說「呀，我吃到硬幣了！」姥姥也祝福小姨說：「看來新的一年妳會財源滾滾！」

　　米亞和艾瑪這下明白了，原來硬幣都藏在餃子裡，吃到有硬幣的餃子就代表新的一年會財運滿滿。「我也要吃到有硬幣的餃子！」米亞說著又夾了一顆餃子。「我也要！」艾瑪給自己又夾了兩顆餃子。

　　米亞吃了十顆餃子後還是沒有吃到有硬幣的，艾瑪也一樣。就這樣，為了能吃到硬幣，米亞和艾瑪比平時多吃了好多餃子，一直吃到肚子都鼓成大西瓜了才肯放棄。

　　「肚子都快撐破了，也沒有吃到帶硬幣的餃子。」米亞失望的說。艾瑪在一旁不停的打飽嗝。

二 吃餃子

「來，小姨今天吃到了兩個帶硬幣的餃子，小姨把一半的財運分給米亞。」說完，小姨送給米亞一枚硬幣。

「舅舅也吃到兩枚硬幣，我也分給艾瑪一個。」就這樣，米亞和艾瑪一人得到了一枚硬幣。

拿到硬幣的艾瑪和米亞非常高興，一整晚她們都將硬幣緊緊握在手裡，生怕硬幣一不小心掉到沙發底下，或是鋼琴後面，又或是爸爸的口袋裡。

11 吃餃子

12晚餐吃鬆餅

　　家附近新開了一家咖啡店，這天放學後，爸爸媽媽帶著米亞和艾瑪在外面散步正巧走到了這家咖啡店門口。「這家咖啡店好漂亮啊！」米亞忍不住感嘆道。

　　的確，店裡面有時髦的桌椅，展示櫃裡擺放著精緻的蛋糕、蛋撻和三明治。就連裡頭的店員都穿著漂亮的制服。這時爸爸提議道：「正好還沒吃晚飯，要不就趁機嘗嘗這家新開的咖啡店，妳們覺得呢？」米亞和艾瑪興奮的不停點頭，就連媽媽也看上去非常期待。

12晚餐吃鬆餅

「歡迎光臨，請問今天想吃點或喝點什麼？」櫃檯的姐姐問。

米亞和艾瑪看著爸爸遞過來的菜單，上面有沙拉、咖哩、濃湯、三明治以及鬆餅。

「決定好要吃什麼了嗎？」爸爸問。米亞和艾瑪早就決定好要吃鬆餅了，想到鬆軟的鬆餅，艾瑪的肚子忍不住發出咕嚕咕嚕的聲音。

「我決定好了！」米亞對爸爸說。「我要一份香草冰淇淋鬆餅，淋上熱熱的楓糖漿。」

「我也決定好了！」艾瑪緊接著說。「我也要一份香草冰淇淋鬆餅，淋上熱熱的楓糖漿！」米亞一聽，馬上阻止艾瑪道，「艾瑪妳不能學我！」

艾瑪有點尷尬了，她大眼睛轉了轉，馬上有了主意，大聲說「我要一份香草冰淇淋鬆餅淋上熱熱的蜂蜜。」

「妳們確定晚飯要吃鬆餅？」媽媽問道。「非常確定。」姐妹倆同時回答。

「那好吧！」爸爸向店員姐姐點了兩份鬆餅，還有媽媽的沙拉以及他自己的三明治，還有一杯咖啡。店員姐姐給了爸爸一個圓形的電子感應器，爸爸說等感應器振動的時候，就可以去櫃檯那拿我們的餐點了。

他們坐在一個有沙發的位置。坐下來後，米亞和艾瑪的視線就沒離開過那個感應器。

「妳猜它什麼時候會震動？」米亞問艾瑪。

「我希望它馬上就震動！」艾瑪回答道。

經過了漫長的等待，感應器終於亮起紅燈並且發出噗滋噗滋的聲響。

「我要去幫忙拿鬆餅！」艾瑪跟著爸爸前去櫃檯。

「我也要！」米亞也從座位上爬下來跟在爸爸身後。父女三人每人手上都端著圓圓的大盤子。

12 晚餐吃鬆餅

「這簡直是世界上第一超級無敵最好吃的鬆餅！」
艾瑪開心的說道，嘴裡還塞滿了鬆餅。米亞也忍不住點
頭表示贊同。這真的是她所吃過最美味的鬆餅。

「我的三明治也非常不錯。」爸爸說。「沙拉醬很
美味。」媽媽也說。

米亞和艾瑪一口氣把盤子裡的三塊鬆餅和一球很大
很圓的冰淇淋都給吃光了。最後她們只能在咖啡店裡多
休息會兒，因為米亞和艾瑪的小肚子已經鼓地跟氣球一
樣圓！

13 爸爸的咖哩

「我宣布，今天的晚餐就由爸爸來做！」爸爸向媽媽和米亞艾瑪宣布。「讓妳們嘗嘗全世界最好吃的咖哩！」說完，爸爸便挺著胸脯走進了廚房。

「對呀，米亞和艾瑪還從來沒有吃過爸爸做的咖哩呢，對吧？」媽媽放下手中的書扭頭問正在專心畫畫的兩姐妹。

「爸爸會做咖哩？」米亞有些不可置信。

「我不喜歡吃辣辣的咖哩。」艾瑪頭也不抬地說。

「妳們一定會愛上我的咖哩！等著瞧！」爸爸從廚房喊道。

沒過多久爸爸的咖哩就出爐了。米亞艾瑪迫不及待的每人盛上了滿滿一碗米飯，然後爸爸又給姊妹倆淋上兩勺熱騰騰的咖哩醬汁。

「好香啊！」連勺子都還沒拿的米亞忍不住舔了一小口碗裡的咖哩。「味道也很不錯！」

「味道怎麼樣？」爸爸端著自己的那碗咖哩坐到兩姐妹對面。

「咖哩有點甜甜的？」米亞有些疑惑的問道。

「妳的舌頭還真靈敏！」爸爸笑著說「那是因為我加了一種特別的材料，妳們要不要猜猜看是什麼？」

「我知道！」嘴裡還塞滿米飯的艾瑪舉手搶答：「我猜你一定加了巧克力！」

「不對，艾瑪答錯了！」爸爸對艾瑪說：「米亞要不要試著猜猜看？」

　　米亞仔細研究碗裡的咖哩醬。裡頭有胡蘿蔔、雞肉、土豆，還有……

　　「這個很像土豆但又不是土豆的是什麼呢？」米亞嘟囔著。

　　「放進嘴裡嘗嘗看。」爸爸鼓勵道。

　　米亞好奇的嘗了一塊。「呀！是蘋果！」米亞驚訝地發現。

「沒錯，就是蘋果！米亞答對了！」爸爸放下手裡的勺子給米亞鼓掌。

「放了蘋果的咖哩？」艾瑪歪頭看向爸爸。

「很奇怪，但是我喜歡！」艾瑪對著爸爸說。

「我也是！咖哩裡放蘋果超酷的！」米亞對著爸爸豎起了一根大拇指。

「我也贊同。」媽媽說：「有蘋果的咖哩非常的好吃。」於是她們每個人都吃完了一大碗咖哩。接著又都吃完了一小碗咖哩。

14 不想再吃咖哩了

　　前天晚上爸爸第一次給米亞和艾瑪做了他獨家的蘋果咖哩。咖哩很美味，米亞和艾瑪也很喜歡吃。只不過爸爸一次煮了滿滿大鍋的咖哩。這已經是她們連著第三天吃咖哩了。米亞和艾瑪感覺她們的皮膚都要變成咖哩的顏色了！

　　「米亞艾瑪，準備吃飯嘍！」媽媽從廚房叫道。

　　「今天晚上吃什麼？」艾瑪期待的問媽媽。

　　「讓我猜猜，該不會還是咖哩吧？」米亞擔憂的問。

　　「是的孩子們，今天晚上我們依然是吃爸爸煮的蘋果咖哩。」媽媽回答。「別忘了爸爸可是煮了整整一大鍋的咖哩。」

　　接著爸爸從廚房裡端出了兩碗咖哩。一碗給米亞，另一碗給艾瑪。

14 不想再吃咖哩了

「香噴噴的咖哩來嘍，大家快開動吧！」爸爸說道。對面坐著的米亞和艾瑪看著眼前的咖哩遲遲不動勺。

「怎麼了？妳們的咖哩有什麼問題嗎？」爸爸問道。

「我們前天晚上吃的什麼？」米亞反問爸爸。

「妳們難道不記得了嗎？」爸爸說。「當然是蘋果咖哩。」

「那我們昨天早上吃的什麼？」這次輪到艾瑪來發問。

「如果我沒記錯的話，應該是蘋果咖哩。」爸爸回答。

「那我們昨天中午吃的什麼？」這回又換米亞來問問題。

「我記得妳們的午餐盒裡裝的應該是炒飯才對。」爸爸說。

米亞與艾瑪

　　「大錯特錯！」艾瑪激動的拍桌子。「還是蘋果咖哩！咖哩！」

　　「啊，是這樣嗎？」爸爸有些訝異。「不過很好吃，對吧？」艾瑪叉著手，眉毛皺的仿佛就要連在一起。

　　「那我們昨天晚上吃的是什麼？」米亞又問。

14 不想再吃咖哩了

「我想應該是全世界第一好吃的蘋果咖哩。」爸爸笑著回答。

「今天早上吃的蘋果咖哩，今天中午又是蘋果咖哩，今天晚上還……」米亞還沒說完，爸爸突然打斷說道「但是今天晚上不一樣。」米亞和艾瑪頓時感到疑惑。擺在自己面前的不是還是蘋果咖哩嗎？到底哪裡不一樣？

「妳們仔細瞧。」爸爸對兩姐妹說。米亞和艾瑪仔細端詳著眼前的咖哩，並沒有看出有任何不同。

「哪裡不一樣。」艾瑪大叫「明明還是蘋果咖哩！」

「難道妳們沒有發現嗎？」爸爸問「我新加了鳳梨！」爸爸興奮的介紹著。「現在妳們不能說它是蘋果咖哩了，因為它是蘋果鳳梨咖哩。」

「哦不！」米亞和艾瑪絕望的大叫。

米亞與艾瑪

14不想再吃咖哩了

15 我不想和妳做朋友了

　　米亞和艾瑪吵架了。兩個人已經一下午都沒有和對方說過一句話。她們各自呆在自己的房間裡，米亞在看書，艾瑪在塗顏色。只不過這次，媽媽也弄不清楚吵架的原因。為了幫姐妹倆快點重歸於好，媽媽先是去了米亞的房間，打算問問米亞這吵架的原因到底是什麼。

　　米亞一個人坐在書桌前畫畫，當媽媽問她為什麼和艾瑪吵架時，米亞只是生氣的說：「我再也不和艾瑪玩了！」媽媽無奈地離開米亞的房間後，又去了艾瑪的房間。艾瑪氣鼓鼓地坐在床邊。媽媽也問了艾瑪同樣的問題：「為什麼和姐姐吵架了呀？」

　　「我就是討厭姐姐！」艾瑪生氣地喊道。

　　這時媽媽把米亞叫到了艾瑪的房間然後說「好了，現在妳們倆一塊跟我說說到底發生了什麼？」媽媽雙手插著腰看著兩姐妹。

　　米亞和艾瑪看著對方卻遲遲不說話。兩個人只是時不時發出「嗯……」的思考聲。

　　「好了，我看出來了，妳們兩個都忘記因為什麼吵架了。」媽媽說：「既然都忘記了，那肯定不是什麼嚴重的事，妳們倆說對不對呢？」

　　米亞和艾瑪安靜的仔細琢磨媽媽的話，最後總結：覺得媽媽說得很有道理，甚至覺得自己有些滑稽，連吵架的原因都不記得了！

15我不想和妳做朋友了

於是在媽媽的見證下，米亞和艾瑪握手和好了。兩個人又在一起愉快的玩起了最喜歡玩的過家家。

16 老照片

「我好無聊啊！」艾瑪從沙發上一點一點滑到地上。

「今天妳想玩點什麼呢？」坐在一旁的米亞問。

「我不知道。」艾瑪回答。

16 老照片

米亞想了想後問道：「過家家？捉迷藏？畫畫？還是捏泥土？」

「這些我都玩膩了！」艾瑪說完，撲通一下躺倒在地上。「我想玩些不一樣的。」

「比如？」米亞問道。

「我想去冒險！」艾瑪突然興奮從地上爬起來：「我們來玩冒險家的遊戲吧！」

「那要怎麼玩？」米亞好奇的問妹妹。

「媽媽的衣帽間裡有　個小箱子妳記得嗎？」艾瑪神秘兮兮地說。

「妳是好奇箱子裡裝的是什麼對吧。」米亞早就猜到妹妹的小心思。

　　「沒錯，就是這個意思。」艾瑪說「我們快開始冒險吧！」說完姊妹倆便自以為偷偷的進入到媽媽的衣帽間，找到了那個小箱子。米亞和艾瑪不知道的是，媽媽也早就發現姊妹倆嘰哩咕嚕的不知道又有什麼壞主意，一直偷偷的跟在她們身後。

　　「妳猜箱子裡會有什麼？」米亞問艾瑪。

　　「我猜會有很多寶藏！像是黃金或者鑽石。」艾瑪頗為興奮地說。

　　兩個人抱著滿滿的好奇心打開了那個神秘的盒子。

16老照片

「居然不是鑽石！只有一堆紙！」艾瑪失望的看著箱子裡的東西。

「是照片。」米亞說，隨後她從盒子裡拿起了一張。「這個女生好漂亮呀，不過這是誰呢？」艾瑪也好奇湊過來：「給我看給我看，我也要看！」

這時媽媽走到兩姐妹身後蹲下來，輕輕點了點她們姊妹倆的肩膀。

「啊！」艾瑪和米亞被嚇了一跳。「妳們兩個在亂翻什麼呢？」

「為什麼妳會有這麼多不認識的女孩的照片？」艾瑪問媽媽。

媽媽笑著回答：「仔細看看，真的不認識照片裡的女孩嗎？」

米亞認真端詳著手裡的照片。忽然，她認出了照片裡的女孩。

「媽媽這是妳嗎？」米亞興奮的問。

米亞與艾瑪

「眞聰明！」媽媽回答「這是媽媽上大學的時候，那時還沒有妳們倆呢。」

「那這個又是誰？」艾瑪舉起另一張照片到媽媽面前。

「這是爸爸年輕的時候呀。」媽媽接過艾瑪手中的照片說道。「妳們看看，裡面還有好多妳們倆小寶寶時候的照片。」

「這裡有一張外星人的照片。」米亞將外星人的照片拿給媽媽看。

媽媽不停地笑「這是妳剛出生的時候，多可愛啊，怎麼會像外星人呢？」

「我的皮膚都皺巴巴而且沒有頭髮，跟外星人一模一樣！」米亞說。

艾瑪這次找到了一張姐妹倆小時候出門旅行的照片，但奇怪的是她完全不記得自己去過照片裡的沙灘，姐姐也不記得了。

16老照片

　　於是媽媽開始給她們講起了那趟旅行的故事。其中有好多路上發生好玩的事，比如說艾瑪因為暈車吐了一路，還有米亞嘴裡吃到沙子，結果一直到第二天早上吃東西嘴裡都會發出咔哧咔哧的聲音。媽媽講的故事聽得米亞和艾瑪不停的咯咯笑。每講完一個故事，米亞或艾瑪總會再遞給媽媽一張照片，讓她講照片背後的故事。就這樣，故事一個接著一個，媽媽一直講直到樓下的爸爸喊三人晚飯做好了。此時的米亞和艾瑪只希望今晚不再吃咖哩。

國家圖書館出版品預行編目資料

米亞與艾瑪 Mia and Emma／陳聖蕾 Mia Chen
著. --初版.--臺中市：白象文化事業有限公司，
2023.01
　　面；　公分
ISBN 978-626-7189-11-5（平裝）
中英對照
863.599　　　　　　　　　　111012760

米亞與艾瑪 Mia and Emma

作　　者　陳聖蕾 Mia Chen
發 行 人　張輝潭
出版發行　白象文化事業有限公司
　　　　　412台中市大里區科技路1號8樓之2（台中軟體園區）
　　　　　出版專線：（04）2496-5995　　傳真：（04）2496-9901
　　　　　401台中市東區和平街228巷44號（經銷部）
　　　　　購書專線：（04）2220-8589　　傳真：（04）2220-8505
專案主編　陳婉婷
出版編印　林榮威、陳逸儒、黃麗穎、水邊、陳婉婷、李婕
設計創意　張禮南、何佳諠
經紀企劃　張輝潭、徐錦淳、廖書湘
經銷推廣　李莉吟、莊博亞、劉育姍、林政泓
行銷宣傳　黃姿虹、沈若瑜
營運管理　林金郎、曾千熏
印　　刷　基盛印刷工場
初版一刷　2023年1月
定　　價　360元

Contents

1 I absolutely, very much need it!

Mum and dad and Emma and I are going for a walk after dinner.

We went to our local supermarket, mum said I can walk around by myself if I take Emma with me.

"I'm going to look for handkerchiefs, I need them for kindergarten." I tell Emma.

She stares at me blankly, so I stare back at her too.

"Well go on then, I haven't got ALL DAY." Emma says.

So, I went about around the store while Emma followed quietly behind me.

I spot a big bin where all the handkerchiefs are stored.

"I can't decide if I want this one with a kitty or this other one with a bow" I say to myself.

I was still choosing between the two handkerchiefs when Emma miraculously disappeared!

I walk around the store looking for Emma.

1 I absolutely, very much need it!

"There you are!" I say, after spotting Emma standing alone in the middle of another aisle.

"I'm getting this." Emma says to me. wrapped tightly in her arms is a water bottle larger than her head.

I say to her "You have to ask mum first."

She rolled her eyes a few times to the right, then a few times to the left, and starts to walk around again.

"Wait for me!" I chase behind her.

She finally stops walking after a few laps around the store.

It looks like she has been looking for mum all this time.

"I'm getting this water bottle." she tells mum. But mum says no.

Tears begin to fill up Emma's eyes and she hugs the bottle even tighter. When mum says to her no once more, she thumps down on the ground and kick and cry and roll and scream. But mum still says no to the water bottle.

So, Emma stands up again and jump and jump and jump until she become so tired, she falls to the floor again. Although her crying never stopped.

Mum finally gives up and got her that big water bottle, and my handkerchief with a bow on it, of course.

Emma came home from school rather grumpy the next day.

She went straight into the kitchen, pulled a stool, stood tip toe on the stool, and pushed her big water bottle all the way to the very back of the cupboard. she pouted her lips as she walks past me and into her room.

"I wonder what's wrong with her." I ask mum curiously. mum laughed, and that made me even more curious.

"Emma's teacher said her big water bottle was way too heavy, and it fell on her face when she tried drinking from it!"

I can't help but giggle a little too.

I went into her room only to find her snuggled up in her bed drinking orange juice out of her old baby bottle.

"I'm never, ever, not ever bringing that water to kindergarten ever again!" Emma said.

Oh Emma.

1 I absolutely, very much need it!

2. I'm the Teacher

"I say we play our absolute favorite game today." I say.

"I bet you know exactly what game I'm talking about." This time I say while smiling at Emma.

"I know what game." Emma reply. "Puzzles!"

"No, not puzzles." I groaned. "We're going to play school!"

"Okay, I like that game too." Emma says.

We need some chairs, a few desks, lots of books and school supplies. Most importantly, we need students.

"I guess I will be the teacher of our classroom today." I say to Emma. "I learned a new dance at school, I can teach the dance."

"I will be the teacher too! My teacher taught me how to twist my bum." Emma says while twisting her bum.

"No, there can't be two teachers in one classroom." I say to Emma. "If we are both teachers, who is going to our student?"

I then say, "I am older than you, so I should be the teacher."
"That's not fair!" Emma stomps her feet and curls up her fists. Her face turns red like a tomato.

"Fine, we can take turns being teachers." I finally decide. We then agree that I would teach dance and counting first, then Emma can teach how to twist bums. But first, we both need to change into something more appropriate for dancing. Princess dresses are perfect.

"Excellent, now we are student and teacher of princess school!" I can't help but twirl in circles, seeing my dress poof up whenever I do so.

"Now, we can begin our class." I announce. "I am going to teach how to dance like a princess. First, you must twirl at least ten times like so." I say as I twirl exactly ten

2. I'm the Teacher

times.

Emma and I twirled until the ceiling start to twirl too. The ceiling kept twirling even when we fall on the floor.

"Now it's time for counting." I say, "we are going to count from one to one hundred, I will count to twenty first, and then you can repeat." So, I count to twenty.

"Now it's your turn Emma."

"One, two, three…" Emma counts with her fingers. But she soon realizes that she doesn't have enough fingers to count to twenty.

"I'm bored with counting now, it's my turn to be the teacher!" Emma says.

"But we are not done counting yet, we just got to twenty." I complain.

"I am the teacher now!" Emma says angrily, her eyebrows come close together. She even crossed her arms to show just how mad she is.

Emma is the teacher now, and she is teaching me how to twist my bum.

"Ok, I've learned it now." I say to Emma after twisting my bum a few times. "I think we should get back to counting now."

"Not fair! I didn't even get to be the teacher for five minutes!" Emma complains.

"I don't want to learn how to twist my bum! It's too silly." I yell back.

"No fighting!" Mum comes in and says. "No fighting, otherwise no one gets to play any more games today."

Mum then says to both of us, "you two are both excellent teachers, why can't you be teachers together?"

"If we are both teachers, who is going to be our students?" I ask mum. Mum smiled then left the room. She returned shortly after with a few of Emma and my stuffies.

2. I'm the Teacher

"Here, Let Mr. Puppy, piggy, and Dolly be your students." Mum says to us as she place our students on their chairs. "I bet that they will be the best students."

"Let's teach them how to twist their bums first, and then we can teach them counting. What do you think?" I ask Emma.

"I think that's just great." Emma answers.

MIA AND EMMA

3. Zoo

Today is the day Emma's preschool class will be performing at the zoo. So, mum and dad and I got to the zoo nice and early right after breakfast. Emma is already at the zoo with her preschool class for final rehearsals before the big show.

"Do you think we will have time to see the koalas and the giraffes before Emma's show?" I ask mum.

"We are here quite early; I suppose we can walk around for a bit before we have to get to the show." Dad answered.

"Perfect! Can we go visit the koalas first?" I ask.

"I don't see why not." Dad smiles.

Mum and dad and I visited many animals at the zoo. I saw the koalas, giraffes, elephants, and even pandas. Dad even got me pudding inside an egg at lunch. I get it every time I come to the zoo. I even saved one for later to give to Emma. After that, it was finally time for Emma's performance to start.

3. Zoo

The music starts playing, and I can see penguins wobble their way on stage.

"Look, that's Emma! She's a penguin!" I say to mum.

the penguins twist and turn and raise their arm and raise their feet. They even twist their bums like how Emma had taught me.

"Emma can't see us, she's falling behind!" I tell mum.

mum tells me how the lights on stage are too bright for Emma to see us, she say I should try waving to her, perhaps she can see me wave.

I wave at the stage eagerly; Emma finally sees me, and she waves back at me.

Emma stopped dancing and instead continues to wave at me.

"Look mum, Emma can see me now!"

"Oh my goodness."

So, I keep waving at Emma, and Emma keeps waving back at me until the curtains were pulled and the show is over.

 3. Zoo

04. The Absolute Worst Day Ever

Mum is on a business trip.

Emma and I are spending an entire week alone with dad at home.

I do not Like it. Not one single bit.

I like it when mum is home. mum knows I like to bring my favorite handkerchief with a bow to kindergarten every day.

Mum knows I like to have my hair in two pig tails for kindergarten.

Mum knows I get to wear my sundress with flowers on it on Fridays.

Most importantly, I get to wake up to warm milk made by mum every morning,

These are all things dad doesn't know.

Friday morning, Emma and I wakes up only to find cold, straight out of the fridge milk.

"This is the worst day ever." I say.

I finish the not-so-good milk and look for dad to help me change. I especially made sure to tell him that today is Friday, which means I get to wear my pretty flower sundress.

But dad put me in pants that are in the most boring grey color and a top with no flowers or glitter on it.

"Can this day get any worse." I wonder.

I then tell dad I like my hair in two pigtails. But dad says he doesn't know how to do pigtails. So instead, he put my hair up in a boring pony tail.

"I can't imagine this day getting any worse." I think to myself.

MIA AND EMMA

04. The Absolute Worst Day Ever

At school, when I look for my handkerchief to dry my hands, instead of my favourite handkerchief with a bow on it, I found only a handkerchief in the ugliest red color inside my pockets.

"This is the absolute worst day ever!"

Dad picks up Emma and I afterschool.
"What's wrong Mia? You look upset." Dad asks me.
"I miss mum." I cried.
I miss warm milk in the morning, I miss pigtails for school, I miss my handkerchief with a bow.

"How about we get some ice-cream?" Dad says.
"Emmmmmm ice-creamm." Emma smiles a big smile.

Dad gets all three of us each a vanilla ice-cream. On our walk home, I notice dad was wearing two different socks on his feet! He is having a rough time with mom away too, just like I am!

I decide today is not the absolute worst day ever.

05. Halloween

It's Halloween, Emma and I are very excited. Everyone gets dressed up at school today,

"I'm wearing a fairy costume this year." I say to Emma. "It's even got wings!"

Emma is wearing her puppy costume. She chose it herself. She can't wait to be a real puppy.

"Can your puppy fly?" I ask Emma.

"Of course I can." Emma answers.

"No, you can't, because you don't have wings, and you don't have a magic wand either." I tease her.

Emma's face turns red and say "I said I can fly! I am a puppy that can fly!"

"Don't be silly, puppies can't fly." I say to Emma "Because you haven't got pixie dust yet."

I waved my fairy wand three times around Emma's head and tell her "Now you can fly, because I just gave you some fairy dust with my magical fairy wand."

Emma is happy now, so I say, "now we can fly together, we will go trick-or-treating flying!"

"I'm ready for candy." Emma said.

Dad took Mia and Emma to school. But they cannot wait to go trick-or-treating tonight!

06. Emma's Fancy Haircut

Mia is staying afterschool today to help her teacher decorate for their class party. Emma is left being very bored at home while mum cooks dinner.

Mum leaves home to pick up Mia a little later. Now Emma is bored more than ever.

Then, a great idea comes to mind. Emma knows just what to do.

She grabs her plastic bowl from the cubby from the kitchen, then gets herself a pair of scissors from dad's study, then she gets her mini mirror from her room.

06. Emma's Fancy Haircut

"I'm home!" I make sure to say it loud enough for Emma to hear. But there was no response.

So, I say it even louder this time "Emma, I'm home now!"

"Busy!" Emma shouted.

"Oh Emma, what have you done!" Mum cried.
"What happened?" I say as I quickly take off my shoes and goes to the living room where mum and Emma is at.

Emma had given herself a new haircut. A perfect square right in the middle of her bangs.

She stares at mum and I as we giggle. "Looks like Emma gave herself a very fancy haircut." Mum says. And we giggle even more.

Emma stare at us until she couldn't help but giggle too, her face turning red like an apple.

"I must make a really good hairstylist." Emma thought to herself.

07. Eggs

Mum made hard boiled eggs for Emma and me to each have two. Mum also says we must finish the eggs before we get to have any cake.

"I hate eating egg yolks." I say, "I feel like I'm eating baby chicks!"

"And I hate egg whites." Emma says, "they are too white."

"What should we do? Mum said no cake unless we eat these eggs!"

Emma starts rolling her eyes around again, that means she's thinking of a plan. I start thinking too, although nothing good comes to mind.

07. Eggs

Suddenly, Emma grabs one of the eggs and separate the egg white from the egg yolk.

"What are you doing?" I ask. But she didn't respond. Soon, Emma has separated the egg whites and the egg yolks from all four eggs.

"I help you eat the egg yolks, and you can help me eat the egg whites." Emma finally says.

"Ohhhhhhhhhhh" I exclaim. That is a great plan.

I ate all the egg whites and Emma ate all the egg yolks. Mum is very happy. But mum did not know about our great plan.

We each got a big piece of strawberry cake. Emma saves the day after all.

08. Mia's Birthday

Today is a very special day. It's my birthday! I love birthdays, I love birthday cake on my birthday, I love singing the birthday song, and most out of all, mum gives me a special birthday present every year!

I can't wait for my birthday party tonight. But first, mum is taking me to the mall to pick up my special birthday present.

"I see barbies everywhere!" I say as I let go of mum's hand. Very soon I find the barbie that is perfect for my special birthday present. It has a barbie doll, a few dresses, and a glittery handbag and a kitten. I even get to have my gift put in a pink bag with a giant pink bow on it. Mum offers to carry it for me, but I want to carry my special birthday present myself.

Then, mum goes into another shop filled with pretty dresses. That's when I spot the most beautiful dress, a dress that would make a very special birthday present!

"Oh noooo! I don't know what to do!" I cried. It was the perfect dress, a dress that would be perfect for a princess to wear. So, I say to mum "I wish I can have this beautiful dress for my birthday present next year."

Mum said of course and promised me that dress for next year's birthday.

08. Mia's Birthday

We arrive at the party at my favorite restaurant. I was still thinking of the dress when suddenly I see a paper bag with a bow drawn on it sitting at my seat.

"Open it! Open it!" Emma comes hopping up and down. I was surprised to see inside the bag was that dress at the mall!

"I chose it for you!" Emma says proudly.

"This is the most perfect birthday ever!" I say to Emma, and we both can't help but spin in circles until we both got so dizzy and fall to the floor.

Later, all my family and friends came to celebrate my birthday with me! We blew out candles on the birthday cake, ate a ton of cake, and had a wonderful time.

09 Baby Chicks

Mum is on the phone with grandma, she sent Emma and I a box with baby chicks! There are four baby chicks in an extra-large cardboard box. Emma and I are beyond excited. We have never had a pet before, and we have never had baby chicks as pets before. We couldn't take our eyes off them.

"I want to touch them." Emma says.

"You have to be veeerrrryyy gentle." I say, "you might hurt them."

Emma brushed the backs of the baby chicks carefully. Suddenly, she grabs a wing and lifts a baby chick high up in the air.

09 Baby Chicks

"Stop it! You're hurting him!" I scream. The chick struggles its way out of Emma's hold and I let out a big sigh of relief.

Dad came home in the evening, and I ask him if we can move the baby chicks into a new home.

"They are covered in their own poop." Emma says to dad.
"Indeed they are." Dad agreed.

Not long after dad appears with a big plastic bin in his hands, and he say to us "Let's make this their new home."

The next morning mum and dad and Emma and I all got panda eyes. The baby chicks were squeaking non-stop throughout the entire night, so none of us could get any sleep. Emma is so sleepy she put on her pants inside out.

Emma and I can't wait to play with the baby chicks after school. So we very quickly took off our shoes and washed our hands.... but the baby chicks are gone! The bin is empty!

"The chicks have escaped!" Emma cried. "They must think we were too loud and they couldn't sleep!" Emma stare at dad to make sure he knows that it was him who made the chicks escape. "It's your snoring." Emma says to dad.

"They didn't escape." Mum tells us. "I took them to them farm today, they will be happier there."

"Why would you do that!" Emma screamed and cried.

"The chicks escaped from the bin this morning and pooped everywhere around the house" mum then says "The chicks are growing up fast, and very soon our house will be too small for them! They will have plenty more room at the farm and much happier too."

"They won't be eaten?" I ask. Mum answer with a smile and say "Of course not! My friend owns the farm, I promise no baby chick is getting eaten. We can go visit them on the weekend if you want."

Emma and I are happy knowing the baby chicks are happy. We even made a pinky promise with mum that we would visit the farm soon.

Emma can't wait to pet a cow.

09 Baby Chicks

10. Flower Market

We are spending the weekend at Grandpa's house. Dad brought Grandpa along with Emma and I to the flower market that takes place every Sunday morning. Grandpa and Emma and I are at the market while dad looks for a space to park the car. There are people everywhere. Emma and I make sure to hold on tight to grandpa's hand in case he gets lost.

"What do we want to look at?" Grandpa ask us.

we slowly walk into the flower market. There are all sorts of different booths, there are ones selling goldfish, there are ones selling dried fruit, there are even ones that sold kites and gnomes!

"I want to go see the goldfish!" Emma says as she tugs Grandpa towards the booth with goldfish. I follow too. Not only did the booth have goldfish, they have mini houses and corals and whales and dolphins made of colorful glass to decorate your fishbowl with!

MIA AND EMMA

"You can each choose one thing you like." Grandpa says to us smiling.

Before I can finish looking through everything there at the booth, Emma has already taken her pick.

"I want this goldfish! The red one with a polka dot around its eyes!" Emma says.

"What does Mia want?" Grandpa turns to me and asks.

Before I can answer, Emma is already dragging Grandpa towards the fish tank where her goldfish was getting swooped out. I finally choose a mini version of a house that looked like our house and made it to the cashier before Grandpa pays.

"That is a very pretty house you got." Grandpa says. I think so too. I think I'm going to put it on my desk at home so I can look at it every day.

Dad finally found somewhere to park the car and found us in the last booth before the flower market ends. Emma and I are each choosing a pot of flowers for grandpa. I chose a pot of pink flowers an Emma chose one with yellow flowers. Grandpa says he is going to plant them in the front yard when we get home.

Before we left dad got all of us each a cup of freshly squeezed guava juice. There was a lot of slurping and spilling on our way home. And laughing, too.

10. Flower Market

11. Dumplings

Today is the annual Chinese lunar new year, which means we are having dumplings for dinner. Mum and Grandma has been working in the kitchen since early in the morning making dumplings for tonight. Emma and I want to help too.

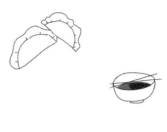

"We want to help too." I say to grandma.

Grandma thought to herself for a moment before she said, "how about you two help me find some coins?"

"Why coins?" Emma asks curiously.

"You will know later." Grandma says mysteriously

Emma and I begin our hunt for coins. Emma found one under the couch, and I found one behind the piano.

"There's my green crayon!"

And yes, we found Emma's missing green crayon as well behind the piano.

The last stop of our hunt was dad's jacket that is hanging by the front door. We found two coins in both of his pockets.

"What are you two looking for?" Dad appears suddenly behind our backs.

"Grandma needed coins, we looked everywhere but we only found these." I say and show dad the couple of coins we found.

Dad then says, "I can help, but first you two have to promise not to go through another person's pocket without asking them."

We nodd in agreement. Dad brought out a ceramic pig from his study and unplugged its belly button. He shakes the pig a few times and some coins fall out.

"So many coins!" I say excitedly.

11. Dumplings

"I'm rich!" Emma exclaims. I made sure to let her know that the money isn't hers to keep, and we are going to give it to grandma. Emma wasn't too happy after that.

"I think that's enough, the coins can barely fit your hands." Dad says. And he is right, we can't fit one more coin in our hands even if we want to.

Dad took Emma and I out for fireworks after we gave the coins to grandma.

It's finally time to eat the dumplings! Plate after plate of fresh, hot dumplings that just came out of the pot are on the dinner table. We can't wait! New Year's dinner is finally starting. I was just finishing my first dumpling when Aunt Lei cried excitedly "There is a coin in my dumpling!" Grandma congratulated her and said, "That means you will have a year filled with fortune!"

"Ohhhhhhhhhhhhhhh" Emma and I looked at each other. That's what the coins were for!

And so, the race begins. Who's going to find a lucky coin in their dumplings.

After eating ten dumplings with a giant balloon belly there still was no coin. neither did Emma find a coin.

"I'm going to have one very unlucky year." I sigh. Emma just keeps burping.

Then, Aunt Lei came over and said, "I got two coins

tonight, I'm giving you one of them, which means I'm sharing half of my luck with you!" Aunt Lei gave me a big gold coin.

Uncle G also got two coins tonight, and he gave one to Emma. And just like that, we each got a coin!

I made sure to keep my coin safe in my pocket in case it gets lost under the couch, or behind the piano, or worse...in dad's pocket.

11. Dumplings

12. Waffles for Dinner

There is a new cafe that opened near our house. One day after school, mum and dad and Emma and I went out for a walk. It just so happens that we walked by the new cafe.

"This cafe is so pretty." I say. Indeed, the cafe has nicely furnished tables and chairs inside, delicious looking cakes, tarts, and sandwiches in the glass showcase. Even the waitresses are dressed in fancy uniforms.

"What do we think about trying the new café for dinner tonight?' Dad ask.

"Yes!" Emma and I say excitedly. Even mum looks excited.

We all take a look at the menu. There are salads, curry, chowders, sandwiches, and waffles.

"Have you two decide on what you want to eat?" Dad asks Emma and I.

Emma and I already knew we wanted waffles. My grumbling tummy has made it very clear it wants waffles.

I tell dad I will have the waffles with vanilla ice-cream drowned in hot maple syrup. Emma orders the same waffles as I did except she wants honey instead.

"Are you sure you want waffles for dinner?" Dad asks us.

"One thousand percent sure." Emma answers for the both of us.

The lady gives us a buzzer and tell us that when the buzzer buzzes, that means our food is ready to get picked up at the counter.

"When do you think it will buzz?" I ask Emma. She doesn't answer but stares hard at the buzzer. Suddenly, she grabs the buzzer and starts to shake it.

"What are you doing?" I ask Emma.

"Maybe it's broken, I'm fixing it." Emma says.

12. Waffles for Dinner

After a looooonnngggg time of shaking the buzzer finally buzzed.

"I fixed it!" Emma says.

Emma and I help bring the food to our table.

"This is the fluffiest most yummy, number one best waffle in the whole world!" Emma says excitedly, her mouth still full with waffle.

"This IS the best waffle!" I agree too.

Dad says his sandwich is good, and mum likes her salad as well.

Emma and I finished all the waffles on our plates along with the big scoop of vanilla ice-cream. We had to stay in the cafe for a bit longer because our stomachs were so full we could barely stand up!

13. Dad's Famous Curry

"I will be making dinner tonight!" Dad announced to Emma and me. "It's time you two get a taste of my famous curry." Then, dad went into the kitchen.

Emma and I have never had dad's famous curry before. We never even knew dad can cook.

"Dad makes curry?" Emma says with a confused face. "I don't like spicey curry."

"You will fall in loooooove with my curry." Dad yells from the kitchen. "Just you wait!"

Then the curry was done. Emma and I each got a big bowl of rice and I made sure to make some room for the curry. Dad gave us each a big scoopful of his famous curry.

"It smells really yummy." I say, and I licked the spoon. "Tastes really yummy too!"

"I knew you would like it!" Dad says.

"Why is it sweet?" I ask dad.

Dad likes the question and ask Emma and I to try and guess the secret ingredient.

13. Dad's Famous Curry

"I know!" Emma says with a mouthful of curry. "You added chocolate!"

Dad say it wasn't chocolate. What might it be then?

I took a closer look at the curry inside my bowl. Carrots, chicken, potatoes, and...

"This looks like a potato, but it isn't a potato." I say to dad while pointing at the mysterious potato lookalike in my bowl.

"Give it a taste." Dad encouraged, and so I did.

"It's an apple!" I found out what the secret ingredient is!

"So, they are not French fries?" Emma is rather confused, but then she says "apple in curry... weird, but I like it!" and ate another big mouthful.

"Apple curry is the coolest!" I tell dad.

"I agree." Mum says. And we all ate our big bowl of curry, and later a little bowl of curry.

13. Dad's Famous Curry

14. No More Curry

The night before last night dad made his famous curry. The curry was very yummy, we like it a lot. But dad made a giant pot of curry, this is our third day eating his famous curry. I feel like I'm about to into curry!

"Time for dinner!" Mum yells from the kitchen.

"What are we having for dinner tonight?" Emma asks mum excitedly.

"Please don't say it's curry, pleaseee." I say to mum.

"Of course it's curry! Tonight, we will be enjoying more of dad's famous apple curry." mum reminds us "don't forget dad made a giant pot of curry, we still have lots left."

Emma and I sat at the dinner table and stared into our bowls of curry.

"What's wrong? Is there anything wrong with the curry?" Dad asks us.

"What did we have the night before yesterday for dinner?" I ask dad.

"Don't you remember? we had my famous apple curry!" Dad says.

MIA AND EMMA

Then Emma asks, "What did we have for breakfast yesterday?"

Dad reply, "If I remember correctly, we had apple curry."

Then I ask, "what did we have for lunch yesterday?"

Dad says, "I remember packing sandwiches in your lunchboxes."

"WRONG!" Emma cried and she pounds on the table. "We had apple curry!"

"Is that right!" Dad seems surprised. "I bet it was delicious though, right?" Emma crossed her arms and fell back into her chair.

So I ask again. "What did we have for dinner last night?"

"I believe we had the number one best curry in the entire world." Dad says.

14. No More Curry

"Curry for breakfast this morning, curry for lunch today, and now curry for dinner..." and before I could finish, dad says "But tonight is different!" Now Emma and I are confused. The brown sauce in our bowls looks just like the curry we have been having for the past two days. What can possibly be different about it?

"Look closely." Dad says. I look closely and so does Emma, but neither of us can spot any difference.
"There's nothing different, it's still apple curry!" Emma is very mad now.

"Didn't you notice?" Dad asks, "I added pineapple slices! now you can't say that it's apple curry, because it is apple pineapple curry!"

"Oh noooooooo!"

15. I Don't Want to Be Your Friend Anymore

Mia and Emma got into a fight. It is a really bad fight. Neither of them has said a single word to another since the beginning of the afternoon. Now Mia is reading quietly in her room, and Emma is drawing in her room. Mum decides to help the two make up, so she is on a mission to find out what really happened.

Mia is sitting in front of her desk reading quietly. Mum asks her what was the reason for their fight? But all angry Mia said was "I'm never, ever playing with Emma ever again!" Mum left Mia's room without an answer and goes to Emma's room next. Emma sits by her bed with her arms crossed. Mum asks her the same question.

"I hate my sister!" Emma says angrily.

Mum still doesn't know what the reason was for their fight. So, mum gets Mia to come to Emma's room and ask the two of them to tell her what they are fighting for.

Mia and Emma face each other and stared and stared and stared. But no words came out. There's only the occasional "emmmmmm" The sound of thinking.

"I think I know it now." Mum says, "You two forgot what you were fighting about!"

"If you have already forgotten, then it means that the fight must have been about anything important, right?"

Mia and Emma couldn't help but agree with what mum said. They even thought that it was quite funny of them for forgetting what they were fighting about!

So, Mia and Emma shake hands and made up. Now they can play their favorite game of puzzles together!

16. An Adventure In Time

"I'm soooooooo booooored." Emma says while sliding down the couch.

"What do you want to do?" I ask her.

"I don't know." Emma reply.

I thought for a moment before suggesting "hide-and-seek? Drawing? Or clay?"

"But I'm bored of those!" And then Emma thumps to the floor. "I want to do something different."

"Like what?" I ask.

"I want to go on an adventure!" Emma is suddenly very excited. "Let's go on an adventure!"

"How do we play that?" I ask curiously. I have never played adventure before.

"Do you remember that that small box in mum's closet?" Emma says mysteriously.

"You're curious to find what's in that box aren't you." I know Emma all too well.

16. An Adventure In Time

She nods and smiles her big smile. And off we went on our adventure to find out what's in that box.

"What do you think is in there?" I ask Emma.

"Treasures, like diamonds and cookies." Emma says excitedly.

We open the box eagerly.

"No cookies?" Emma can't believe mum wasn't hiding cookies in her closet.

"They are pictures, look!" I say to Emma. I show her the picture I have in my hand. "She's so pretty."

"Let me see, let me see!" Emma grabs the picture from my hand and looks at it closely.

Before we even got a chance figure out who the pretty lady in the picture was, mum finds us sneaking around in her closet.

MIA AND EMMA

"Why do you have a picture of a girl we don't know?" I ask mum.

Mum laughs and tells us to look at the picture again. So, I took a more careful look at the picture and.... "It's mum!" I exclaim.

"That's right! This is a picture of me when I was younger and still in school." Mum says.

"Who is this?" Emma raises another picture for mum to see.

"That's dad from when he was in school." Mum explains to us. "Look, there are pictures in here of when you two were babies."

"There's a picture of an alien!" I show to mum the picture I found.

16. An Adventure In Time

Mum couldn't stop laughing. "This is you when you when you were born, how can you call yourself an alien! Look at how cute you were!"

"My skin is wrinkly, and I have no hair. I look just like an alien." I explain to mum.

Then Emma found another picture of a vacation from when they were younger, but she just couldn't remember ever going to that beach before. I can't remember either. So, mum told us all about the trip. Mum even told us funny stories that happened on that trip, like how Emma got carsick and was throwing up the entire car ride, and how I got sand in my mouth so whenever I eat something it was always crunchy. The stories made Emma and I laugh until our stomachs hurt. Emma and I keep passing pictures to mum for her to tell us about the stories behind them, until dad calls us for dinner from downstairs. Emma and I hope dearly that we will not behaving curry again tonight.